Good Game

Written by Megan Borgert-Spaniol

Illustrated by Jeff Crowther

GRL Consultants, Diane Craig and Monica Marx,
Certified Literacy Specialists

Lerner Publications ◆ Minneapolis

Note from a GRL Consultant
This Pull Ahead leveled book has been carefully designed for beginning readers.
A team of guided reading literacy experts has reviewed and leveled the book to
ensure readers pull ahead and experience success.

Lerner Publications Company
An imprint of Lerner Publishing Group, Inc.
241 First Avenue North
Minneapolis, MN 55401 USA

For reading levels and more information, look up this title at www.lernerbooks.com.

Main body text set in Mikado 24/41
Typeface provided by Hannes von Doehren.

The images in this book are used with the permission of: Jeff Crowther

Library of Congress Cataloging-in-Publication Data

Names: Borgert-Spaniol, Megan, 1989- author. | Crowther, Jeff, illustrator.
Title: Good game / Written by Megan Borgert-Spaniol ; Illustrated by Jeff Crowther.
Description: Minneapolis : Lerner Publications, [2022] | Series: Be a good sport (pull ahead
    readers people smarts - fiction) | Includes index. | Audience: Ages 4–7 | Audience:
    Grades K–1 | Summary: "The red and blue team are playing each other. After the game,
    players on the blue team demonstrate what it means to be a good winner. Pairs with the
    nonfiction title Winning Well"— Provided by publisher.
Identifiers: LCCN 2021010313 (print) | LCCN 2021010314 (ebook) | ISBN 9781728440965
    (library binding) | ISBN 9781728444369 (ebook)
Subjects: LCSH: Sportsmanship—Juvenile literature.
Classification: LCC GV706.3 .B66 2022 (print) | LCC GV706.3 (ebook) | DDC 175—dc23

LC record available at https://lccn.loc.gov/2021010313
LC ebook record available at https://lccn.loc.gov/2021010314

Manufactured in the United States of America
1 – CG – 12/15/21

Table of Contents

Good Game

The blue team played the red team.

"I hope we win,"
said the blue team.

"I hope we win,"
said the red team.

The blue team won
the game.

"Good game!" they said.

The blue team gave snacks to the red team.
The two teams ate together.

How do you show you are a good sport when you win?

Did You See It?

bat

donuts

helmet

Index